CW00840921

A SIENA BOOK

Siena is an imprint of Parragon Books
Published by Parragon Book Service Ltd,
Units 13 - 17, Avonbridge Trading Estate,
Atlantic Road, Avonmouth, Bristol BS11 9QD

Original concept by Julian Tucki • Improved by Guy Parr
Developed by Caroline Repchuk and Dug Steer

Produced by The Templar Company plc,
Pippbrook Mill, London Road, Dorking, Surrey RH4 1JE

Copyright © 1996 Parragon Book Service Ltd

Edited by Caroline Repchuk
Designed by Janie Louise Hunt

Printed and bound in Italy

ISBN 0-75251-313-3

GRANDMA'S
Strawberry
Surprise

ILLUSTRATED BY STEPHANIE BOEY

WRITTEN BY DUGALD STEER

SIENA

Grandma was very proud
of the delicious jams she made.

All of the Jam Pandas had their own
favourite flavour of jam. Grandma's was
strawberry. There was nothing she liked
more than having a nice cup of strawberry
tea, with a strawberry jam sandwich.

7

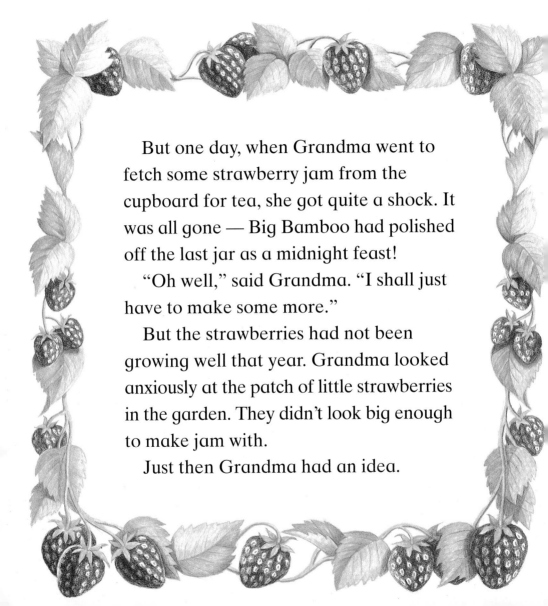

But one day, when Grandma went to fetch some strawberry jam from the cupboard for tea, she got quite a shock. It was all gone — Big Bamboo had polished off the last jar as a midnight feast!

"Oh well," said Grandma. "I shall just have to make some more."

But the strawberries had not been growing well that year. Grandma looked anxiously at the patch of little strawberries in the garden. They didn't look big enough to make jam with.

Just then Grandma had an idea.

In the kitchen, Grandma got out her special book. It was very old. It had been given to her by her Great-Grandma. It might even have belonged to her Great-Great-Grandma.

She searched through the dusty pages until she found what she was looking for. It was a recipe for a magic growing potion. Grandma decided to make some to put on the little strawberries in the garden.

Soon Grandma was busy preparing the magic potion.

She was so busy that she didn't notice that Big Bamboo had eaten one of the secret ingredients while she wasn't looking.

When the potion was ready Grandma put it in a watering can and went outside.

13

In the garden, Peaches and Plum
helped Grandma to water the
strawberries with the special potion.
"What will it do?" they asked.
"It will make the strawberries grow
big and juicy," said Grandma.
"Mmm," said Big Bamboo.
"It smells delicious. Can I try some?"
"Certainly not!" said Grandma.
Big Bamboo was quite big
enough already!

15

Nothing happened to the strawberries
all that day. Peaches and Plum kept going
to look at them just in case.

But that night something
very strange happened.
The strawberries started to grow.

And grow!

When Grandma went into the garden the next day the strawberries were bigger than wheelbarrows!

"Jumping Jamspoons!" she said. "That wasn't supposed to happen! I must have forgotten something."

Big Bamboo blushed as he realised he had eaten the missing ingredient.

Grandma couldn't pick the enormous strawberries to make them into jam. She couldn't even lift them! Neither could Ma or the twins. Not even Pa and Big Bamboo could lift them, though they tried and tried. Poor Grandma didn't know what to do. She couldn't bear to waste all those lovely strawberries.

Then she had another idea.

She told Peaches and Plum that she had a special errand for them to do.

The next day Peaches and Plum visited all the Jam Pandas' friends to invite them to a Spring Strawberry Feast that afternoon, in the garden of Tumbledown Cottage.

And Pa went to the farm to get
a whole wheelbarrowful of cream!

All of their friends came to
the feast.

Everyone agreed it was the
scrummiest Spring Strawberry
Feast they had ever been to.

"These strawberries are
delicious," chuckled Grandma.
"But I think I'll leave nature to
do the growing next time!"

Big Bamboo didn't say
anything.

He was busy eating
strawberries and cream, and
wondering whether there was
any magic potion left that he
could use on his blackcurrants!

• THE END •